A MAGIC EYE FOR IDA

A MAGIC EYE FOR IDA

KAY CHORAO

The Seabury Press
New York

I DA lived with her mother, who was an artist.

Ida's father had moved away so long ago that the only memory Ida had of him was the funny way he dipped celery in butter.

Sometimes Ida crept into her mother's studio and sang a little song:

"I am sitting good as gold
And I wasn't even told
to."

But Ida's mother didn't seem to notice Ida at all.

Ida also lived with her brother, Fred, who wrote long letters to movie stars.

Fred sometimes practiced his barbells and let Ida help.

But mostly he yelled, "Mom, make her get out!"

And that meant Ida.

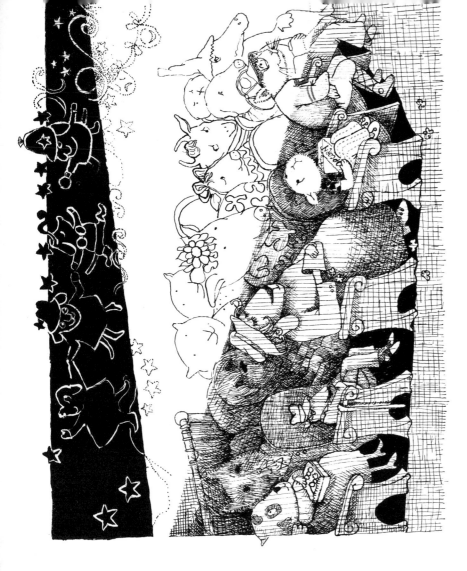

On weekends Fred took Ida to the movies.
Ida would have preferred digging worms in the park, but
Fred said, "No, there's a good movie showing."

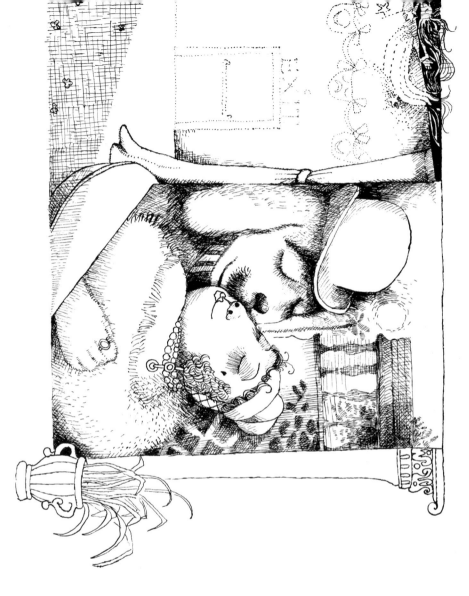

So Ida wiggled in her seat and looked at the glow-in-the-
dark pictures on the movie theater walls.

She wished that Fred would feel sorry for her because she
was so bored.

But Fred enjoyed the movies too much to notice.

During the week, Ida went to school, where she watched Miss Stumpie rap the blackboard with her pointer. Miss Stumpie believed in tidy lines, being a good citizen, flash cards, and zipping lips.

"Who is prepared for show-and-tell?" Miss Stumpie asked one day.

Ida could feel Miss Stumpie's eyes looking at her, like headlights on a scary truck. She slid down in her seat.

"Me, me, me," yelled Alfred.

"Me, me, me," yelled Rudy.

"Next time zipper your lips and raise your paws," snapped Miss Stumpie.

Ida peeped into her duffel bag at Clarence, her doll. She wanted to show him to the class.

But Miss Stumpie called on Yolanda before Ida could raise her paw.

Yolanda was always prepared. She was a good citizen and she kept her feet together so that the lace in her socks made a frilly little circle.

Yolanda raised her voice so the back of the class could hear. "Today I brought my dolly-wetsy-bye. She goes to sleep. She drinks from a bottle. And she wets her pants."

Everyone giggled. The boys poked each other.

"That will do," said Miss Stumpie.

Ida looked at Clarence.

After seeing Yolanda's beautiful doll, everyone would laugh at Clarence. His face was a little orange where Ida had tried to feed him spaghetti with meat sauce. And his hat didn't even come off.

So Ida pushed Clarence to the bottom of her duffel bag and snapped the flap.

At recess Ida asked Yolanda, "Can I play with your dolly?"

"After me and Maude finish," said Yolanda, doing a shuffle-shuffle-shuffle tap step with her Mary Jane shoes.

"She is beautiful," said Ida.

"Oh, she is nothing. I have thirty-two story book dollies on whatnot shelves. You should see *them*."

"I never saw thirty two dollies all at once," said Ida.

"You would at 762 Slipperhouse Street, where I live," said Yolanda. She giggled and skipped away with some more tippy-tap steps.

Ida watched Yolanda and Maude tie a Sunday hanky on the dolly's head. She wished that she could dress Clarence up, but she knew that an elephant in a bowler hat would look silly in doll clothes.

So Ida sat all alone, just hugging Clarence.

When Maude saw Clarence she poked Yolanda.

"If you need a *real* dolly come to 726 Slipperhouse Street," said Yolanda grandly.

Then Maude and Yolanda giggled and ran off, holding their stomachs.

After school Ida ran all the way home.

Sometimes when Ida felt terrible, Ida's mother gave her a kiss and slipped a penny in her pocket. But today Mama was painting.

"Mama, Mama," yelled Ida. "I want a dolly-wetsy-bye."

"There are pretzel rods in the cupboard," said Ida's mother, not looking up.

"*I want a new doll,*" yelled Ida.

"All right, dear. Fred will reach them for you," said Ida's mother.

"Tell her to quit yelling," said Fred, poking his head in the door.

"NO ONE LISTENS TO ME," screamed Ida. Then she ran to her room.

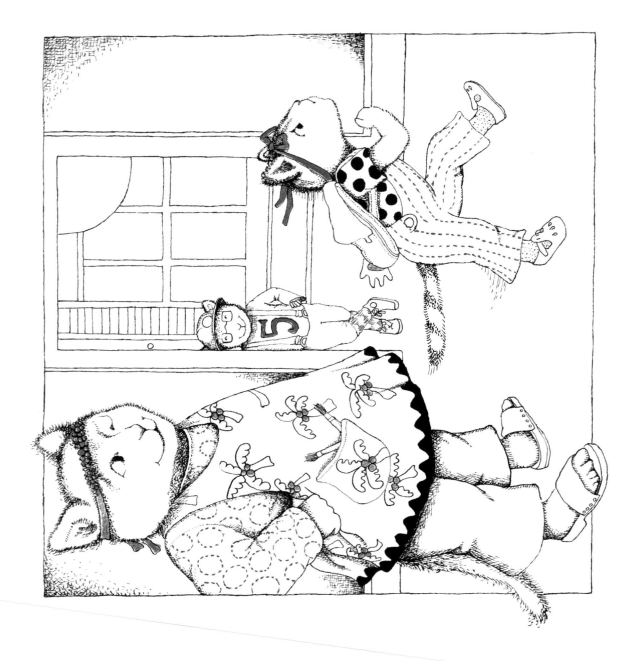

She threw Clarence on her bed and packed her duffel bag with pajamas and some tutti-frutti gum.

"I'm running away," yelled Ida.

Her mother winked at Fred.

"I'm *really* going," said Ida. And she stomped right out the door.

"They don't believe me," said Ida. "They'll see."

She rode the elevator to the first floor.

Then she walked to the subway.

No one noticed her slip under the turnstile.

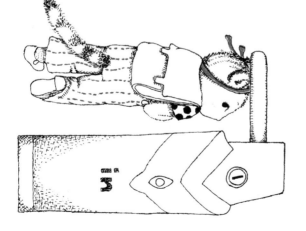

Ida rode the subway train uptown toward Slipperhouse Street.

The train bumped and screeched over the tracks, but Ida smiled a little to herself.

"At Slipperhouse Street
Who will I meet?
A whole bunch of dollies
With shiny new teeth,"

sang Ida.

When the train reached Slipperhouse Street, Ida looked around.

"I don't remember Yolanda's house number," she wailed.

"Are you lost, little girl?" asked a lady.

"I'm not telling," said Ida, and she ran away.

She ran up the stairs and onto the street, where she bumped into some boys playing stickball.

"Who gave you the right to come crashing in here?" yelled a mean-looking boy.

"Get lost or we'll tie your tail to a bus," said another boy. Ida didn't wait to hear more. She ran right across the street without looking.

Some cars beeped at Ida because she had crossed against a red light.

"Never do that!" roared a taxi driver.

"I want Yolanda. I want MAMA," cried Ida.

Signs and lights blinked all around. Through her tears everything was a big blur. But when Ida turned a corner . . .

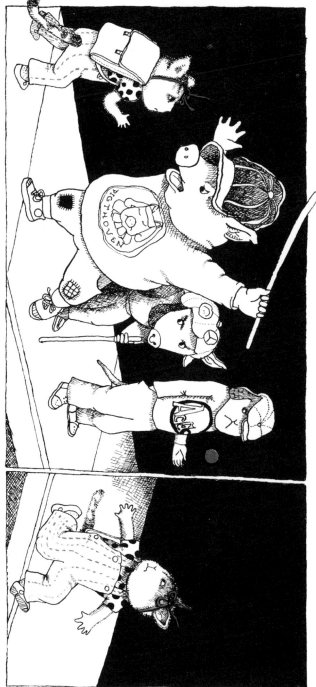

. . . there was an EYE.

"Eeeeeeeks," squealed Ida.

The eye followed her when she walked by.

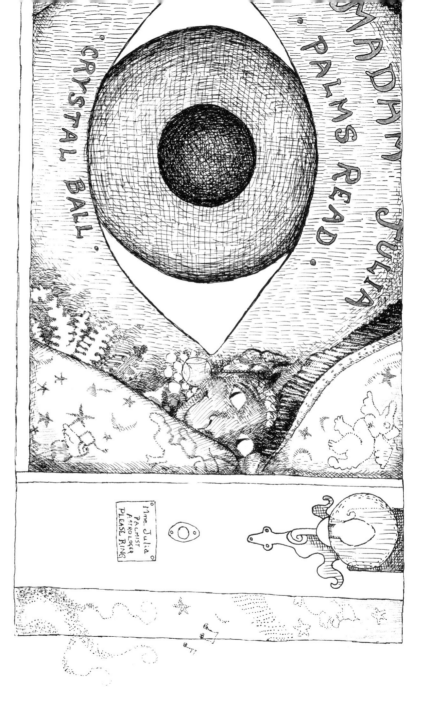

Madam Julia opened her door. "Hello," she said. "Are you lost, dear?"

"I'm not telling," said Ida.

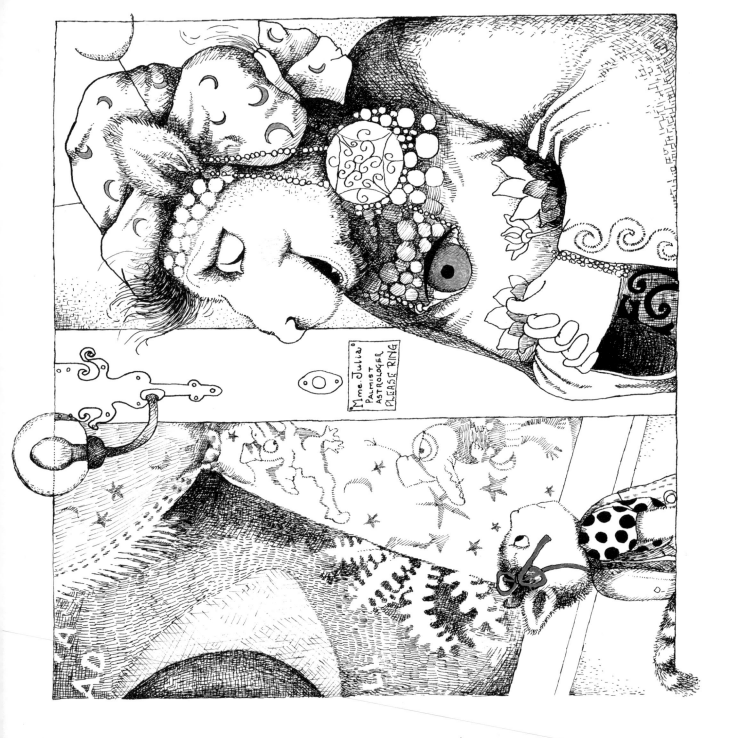

Little feathers of smoke drifted out from Madam Julia's shop. They smelled a little like Mama's dried-up perfume bottles. From inside some music tinkled in a way that made Ida think of snakes slipping and sliding over strange instruments. Madam Julia was part of the music herself. She tinkled all over with gold coins and bangles and things.

"I really should run away," thought Ida.

"Come in and I will read your palm," said Madam Julia.

"My palms are all empty," said Ida suspiciously.

But Madam Julia parted some drapes decorated with dragons and fringe.

Ida was curious. She went inside.

"Ah-ha!" said Madam Julia, looking at Ida's paw. "I see you have bravery and curiosity, and maybe a little temper? And I see something very special."

"Where? I don't see," said Ida, peering at her paw.

"Madam Julia has magic eyes. They see many things about you in the little roads and lines in your palm."

"Well, they are wrong. I'm not special. I'm just Ida and no one ever pays any attention to me, not even Fred or Mama. That is why I am running away to Yolanda's house."

"And who is this Yolanda?" asked Madam Julia.

"She is a girl in my class at school. She wears fancy dresses and she takes tap lessons and she has a dolly-wetsy-bye."

"She sounds a little dull to me," said Madam Julia, shaking her head and making her earrings jingle.

"I know," giggled Ida, "but she has thirty-two story book dollies."

Madam Julia laughed. "So you like Yolanda's dolls, not Yolanda?"

"But if Yolanda traded me a dolly for some tutti-frutti gum, then kids would like me and play with me."

"You mean, they would play with your dolly," said Madam Julia.

Ida thought a minute. "I guess you are right."

She sniffed the sweet-smelling smoke. The strange tin-kling music made her think of a poem.

"I am just a plain old Ida
And my favorite food is fish.
I like it almost any way
Served in a plastic dish.
But now I'm feeling sad and glum,
So sad and bad and glum.
I wouldn't even want to chew
My tutti-frutti gum."

"Bravo!" shouted Madam Julia, clapping her paws.
The music tinkled happily and so did the gold bangles on Madam Julia.
Ida smiled . . . a little.

"Oh, my Mama paints and paints,
'Til you'd think she'd get the faints.
It is such an awful bore,
I could snore and snore and snore,"

sang Ida in a brighter voice.

Madam Julia grabbed a tambourine. With all her gold bangles jingling, she beat out a rhythm and twirled and whirled around the room, repeating Ida's songs. Ida followed, imitating Yolanda's way of tip-tapping her feet.

Then puffing and laughing they slid onto their chairs.

"You see?" Madam Julia said. "You are a poet! The magic eyes of Julia could see something special about you from the beginning. You made me laugh and sing and even dance!"

Ida smiled at Madam Julia. She guessed that Madam Julia had been right after all.

To celebrate, Madam Julia brewed a pot of tea that smelled nicely of mint leaves. This tea didn't have bags with little scraps of paper hanging over the pot, like Mama's.

"There are real leaves in your tea," said Ida, stirring her cup the way Madam Julia stirred hers.

"Of course," said Madam Julia.

And they sipped their tea in a happy quiet way until it was all gone.

"I think maybe I should go now," said Ida.

"To Yolanda's house?" asked Madam Julia.

"No, I don't need Yolanda. I want to go home and see Mama and Fred."

"You are quite right," said Madam Julia. "I will drive you home right away."

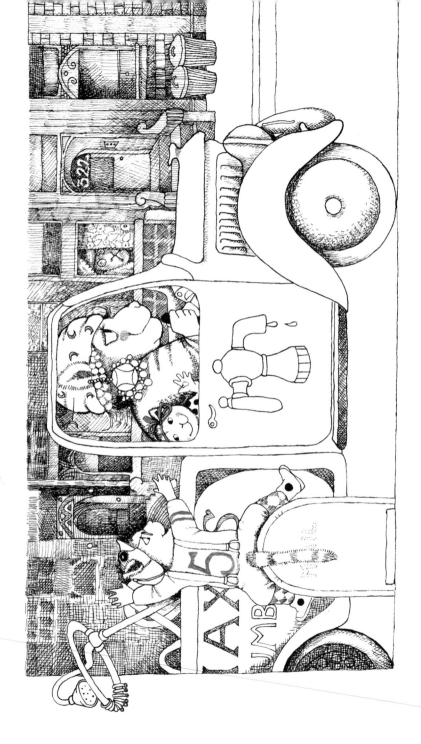

So Madam Julia borrowed her husband's truck and drove Ida home.

They found Fred sitting on the mailbox, and Ida was glad to see him.

"You're going to get it, Ida," he yelled. But he was glad to see her, even so.

"Oh, oh," said Ida, hurrying out of the truck.

Madam Julia looked down at Ida. "Before you go, I want you to have this. It will remind you of the day you made me laugh and dance and sing."

She took off a necklace and slipped it around Ida's neck.

"This is a magic eye, all your own," she said.

"A MAGIC EYE! Thank you. Thank you for everything," said Ida, watching Madam Julia drive away.

"Look, Fred, I've got a magic eye," said Ida, skipping up the steps of her building.

"Uh-hum," said Fred. But Ida could see that he was really thinking, "she's going to get it."

"I'm going to get it. I'm going to get it," thought Ida.

The thump-thump of her mother's footsteps matched the thump in Ida's heart.

The door opened.

"Ida, where have you been! I've been so worried!" cried Ida's mother.

She picked Ida up and squeezed her happily.

"Please never run away again," she whispered.

"All right. But I got a magic eye," whispered Ida.

"A magic eye for Ida," said her mother. "Tell us all about it."

So Ida told Fred and Mama, and even Clarence, all about it.

And they *really* listened, except Clarence, whose ears were badly chewed from the days when Ida was cutting teeth.

The next day Ida took her magic eye to school. Everyone pushed and shoved to be first in line to see it.

Miss Stumpie yelled, "Keep the line tidy."

"And your paws at your side-y," rhymed Ida to herself. Yolanda ripped her Tuesday hanky in the scuffle.

As for Ida . . .

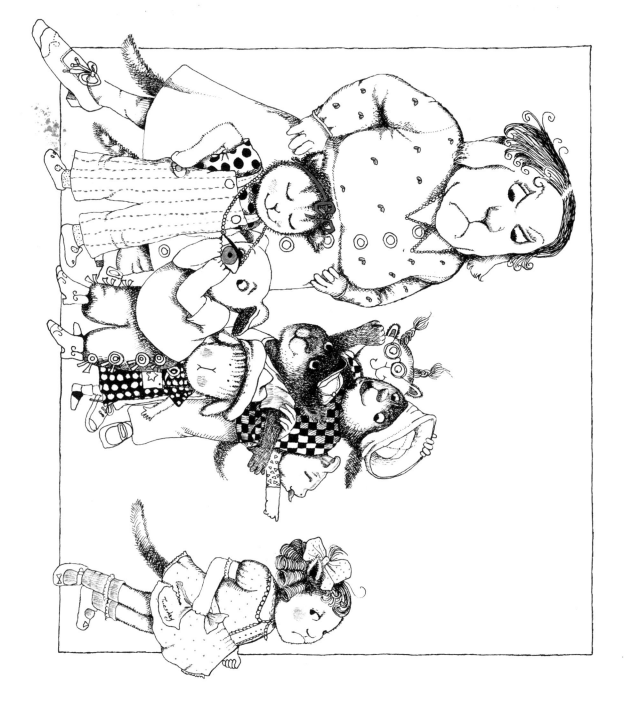

. . . she knew where a lady with *real* magic eyes lived. But she wouldn't tell anyone where.